Justine
1988

A
CHRISTMAS
TREASURY

A
CHRISTMAS
TREASURY

Compiled by Sam Elder

HARPER & ROW, PUBLISHERS, New York

Cambridge, Philadelphia, San Francisco,

1817 London, Mexico City, Sao Paulo, Sydney

Compilation copyright © Sam Elder, 1985

First published in Great Britain by
Orbis Publishing Limited, London

Library of Congress Cataloging in Publication Data
Main entry under title:

A Christmas treasury.

   1. Christmas—Literary collections. 2. English
literature. 3. American literature. I. Elder, Sam.
PR1111.C53C52   1985   820'.8'033   85-42564
ISBN 0-06-015455-1

Printed in Spain by Printer I.G.S.A. Barcelona
D.L.B.: 21208-1985

Contents

Christmas Pie

Lo! now is come our joyfull'st feast!
Let every man be jolly;
Each room with ivy leaves is dressed,
And every post with holly.
Now all our neighbours' chimneys smoke,
And Christmas blocks are burning;
Their ovens they with bakemeats choke,
And all their spits are turning.
Without the door let sorrow lie,
And if for cold it hap to die,
We'll bury it in a Christmas pie,
And ever more be merry.

GEORGE WITHER

Let not Roast Beef be carelessly passed by
At CHRISTMAS hold him in esteem most high

Goose for the Cratchits

Mrs Cratchit made the gravy (ready beforehand in a little saucepan) hissing hot; Master Peter mashed the potatoes with incredible vigour; Miss Belinda sweetened up the apple-sauce; Martha dusted the hot plates; Bob took Tiny Tim beside him in a tiny corner at the table; the two young Cratchits set chairs for everybody, not forgetting themselves, and mounting guard upon their posts, crammed spoons into their mouths, lest they should shriek for goose before their turn came to be helped. At last the dishes were set on, and grace was said. It was succeeded by a breathless pause, as Mrs Cratchit, looking slowly all along the carving-knife, prepared to plunge it in the breast; but when she did, and when the long expected gush of stuffing issued forth, one murmur of delight arose all round the board, and even Tiny Tim, excited by the two young Cratchits, beat on the table with the handle of his knife, and feebly cried Hurrah!

There never was such a goose. Bob said he didn't believe there ever was such a goose cooked.... Eked out by the apple-sauce and mashed potatoes, it was a sufficient dinner for the whole family; indeed, as Mrs Cratchit said with great delight (surveying one small atom of a bone upon the dish), they hadn't ate it all at last! Yet every one had had enough, and the youngest Cratchits in particular, were steeped in sage and onion to the eyebrows!

CHARLES DICKENS

Christmas in Cornwall

In other places they have snow
And holly berries in a row
And crowded shops and cellophane
And Waits who shiver in the lane.

In Cornwall on the festal day
The sun shines brightly on the spray
Driving in pale transparency
At grey-brown cliffs from blue-green sea.

I never dreamed, as snug we sat
With Christmas tree and paper hat,
And all the joys that children bring,
Of climes where Christmas comes like Spring.

Once it was well; but now it's done...
A Christmas feast set out for *one*?
It does no good to mourn the past
Or claim that family bonds should last.

So down to Cornwall I will go,
Where salt plumes on the west winds blow,
To celebrate the Day alone
With gulls and larks and foam and sun.

ROSALIND WADE

With the Season's Greetings.

A Childhood Expedition

Queenie wades the stream first, paddles across barking complaints at the swiftness of the current, the pneumonia-making coldness of it. We follow, holding our shoes and equipment (a hatchet, a burlap sack) above our heads....On the farther shore, Queenie shakes herself and trembles. My friend shivers, too: not with cold but enthusiasm. One of her hat's ragged roses sheds a petal as she lifts her head and inhales the pine-heavy air. 'We're almost there; can you smell it, Buddy?' she says, as though we were approaching an ocean.

And, indeed, it is a kind of ocean. Scented acres of holiday trees, prickly-leafed holly. Red berries shiny as Chinese bells: black crows swoop upon them screaming. Having stuffed our burlap sacks with enough greenery and crimson to garland a dozen windows, we set about choosing a tree. 'It should be,' muses my friend, 'twice as tall as a boy. So a boy can't steal the star.' The one we pick is twice as tall as me. A brave handsome brute that survives thirty hatchet strokes before it keels with a cracking rending cry. Lugging it like a kill, we commence the long trek out. Every few yards we abandon the struggle, sit down and pant. But we have the strength of triumphant huntsmen; that and the tree's virile, icy perfume revive us, goad us on....My friend is sly and noncommittal when passers-by praise the treasure perched in our buggy: what a fine tree and where did it come from? 'Yonderways,' she murmurs vaguely. Once a car stops and the rich

mill owner's lazy wife leans out and whines: 'Giveya two-bits cash for that ol tree.' Ordinarily my friend is afraid of saying no; but on this occasion she promptly shakes her head: 'We wouldn't take a dollar.' The mill owner's wife persists. 'A dollar, my foot! Fifty cents. That's my last offer. Goodness, woman, you can get another one.' In answer, my friend gently reflects: 'I doubt it. There's never two of anything.'

TRUMAN CAPOTE

The Computer's First Christmas Card

jollymerry
hollyberry
jollyberry
merryholly
happyjolly
jollyjelly
jellybelly
bellymerry
hollyheppy
jollyMolly
marryJerry
merryHarry
hoppyBarry
heppyJarry
boppyheppy
berryjorry
jorryjolly
moppyjelly
Mollymerry
Jerryjolly
bellyboppy
jorryhoppy
hollymoppy
Barrymerry
Jarryhappy
happyboppy
boppyjolly
jollymerry
merrymerry
merrymerry
merryChris
ammerryasa
Chrismerry
asMERRYCHR
YSANTHEMUM

EDWIN MORGAN

14

Christmas Quiz

1 Christmas Present. In what novel is one first mentioned?

2 One of Shakespeare's plays refers to the Christmas season in its title, while another mentions Christmas in the first scene. Name the plays.

3 What gastronomic treat offered at Christmas derives its name from the Sanskrit word for 'five'?

4 It seems the wrong part of the Bible, so what was the occasion when extracts of the Book of Genesis were read out over the radio on Christmas Eve, 1968?

5 In what way is the month of Christmas incorrectly named?

6 What part of the traditional Christmas fare seems falsely to claim its origins are in the Old World and not in the New?

7 Who has chronological priority: Clement C. Moore or George R. Sims?

8 In a Christmas pudding, what significance is meant to be provided by the implanted coins, the flaming brandy and the spicy recipe?

9 Its charms can provide the ingredients for a happy holiday. How?

The answers are on page 48.

MICHAEL EASTHER

Wassail, Wassail, all Over the Town

Wassail, wassail, all over the town!
Our toast it is white, and our ale it is brown,
Our bowl it is made of the white maple tree:
With the wassailing bowl we'll drink to thee.

So here is to Cherry and to his right cheek,
Pray God send our master a good piece of beef,
And a good piece of beef that may we all see;
With the wassailing bowl we'll drink to thee.

And here is to Dobbin and to his right eye,
Pray God send our master a good Christmas pie,
And a good Christmas pie that may we all see;
With our wassailing bowl we'll drink to thee.

So here is to Broad May and to her broad horn,
May God send our master a good crop of corn,
And a good crop of corn that may we all see;
With the wassailing bowl we'll drink to thee.

And here is to Fillpail and to her left ear,
Pray God send our master a happy New Year,
And a happy New Year as e'er he did see;
With our wassailing bowl we'll drink to thee.

And here is to Colly and to her long tail,
Pray God send our master he never may fail
A bowl of strong beer; I pray you draw near,
And our jolly wassail it's then you shall hear.

Come, butler, come fill us a bowl of the best,
Then we hope that your soul in heaven may rest;
But if you do draw us a bowl of the small,
May the devil take butler, bowl and all.

Then here's to the maid in the lily white smock,
Who tripped to the door and slipped back the lock,
Who tripped to the door and pulled back the pin,
For to let these jolly wassailers in.

TRADITIONAL GLOUCESTERSHIRE CAROL

Days of Delight

Sunday, Christmas Day 1870
As I lay awake praying in the early morning I thought I heard a sound of distant bells. It was an intense frost. I sat down in my bath upon a sheet of thick ice which broke in the middle into large pieces whilst sharp points and jagged edges stuck all round the sides of the tub like chevaux de frise, not particularly comforting to the naked thighs and loins, for the keen ice cut like broken glass. The ice water stung and scorched like fire. I had to collect the floating pieces of ice and pile them on a chair before I could use the sponge and then I had to thaw the sponge in my hands for it was a mass of ice. The morning was most brilliant. Walked to the Sunday School with Gibbins and the road sparkled with millions of rainbows, the seven colours gleaming in every glittering point of hoar frost. The Church was very cold in spite of two roaring stove fires. Mr. V. preached and went to Bettws.

Monday, 26 December
Much warmer and almost a thaw. Left Clyro at 11am.

At Chippenham my father and John were on the platform. After dinner we opened a hamper of game sent by the Venables, and found in it a pheasant, a hare, a brace of rabbits, a brace of woodcocks, and a turkey. Just like them, and their constant kindness.

REV FRANCIS KILVERT

Xmas Wishes.

With laughter and fun
May your Xmas abound,
And heartiest greetings
Make the air resound.

The Nativity

And it came to pass in those days, that there went out a decree from Caesar Augustus, that all the world should be taxed.

And this taxing was first made when Cyrenius was governor of Syria.

And all went to be taxed, every one into his own city.

And Joseph also went up from Galilee, out of the city of Nazareth, into Judaea, unto the city of David, which is called Bethlehem (because he was of the house and lineage of David)

To be taxed with Mary his espoused wife, being great with child.

And so it was, that, while they were there, the days were accomplished that she should be delivered.

And she brought forth her firstborn son, and wrapped him in swaddling clothes, and laid him in a manger; because there was no room for them in the inn.

ST LUKE CHAPTER 2 VERSES 1-7

Carol of the Brown King

Of the three Wise Men
Who came to the King,
One was a brown man,
So they sing.

Of the three Wise Men
Who followed the Star,
One was a brown king
From afar.

They brought fine gifts
Of spices and gold
In jeweled boxes
Of beauty untold.

Unto His humble
Manger they came
And bowed their heads
In Jesus' name.

Three Wise Men,
One dark like me –
Part of His
Nativity.

LANGSTON HUGHES

A Child of the Snows

There is heard a hymn when the panes are dim,
And never before or again,
When the nights are strong with a darkness long,
And the dark is alive with rain.

Never we know but in sleet and in snow,
The place where the great fires are,
That the midst of the earth is a raging mirth
And the heart of the earth a star.

And at night we win to the ancient inn
Where the child in the frost is furled,
We follow the feet where all souls meet
At the inn at the end of the world.

The gods lie dead where the leaves lie red,
For the flame of the sun is flown,
The gods lie cold where the leaves lie gold,
And a Child comes forth alone.

G. K. CHESTERTON

Drinks of the Season

Mistletoe Mull

1 bottle inexpensive Burgundy	1 stick cinnamon
2 cups (1 US pint) water	4 cloves
1 cup granulated sugar	2 lemons thinly sliced

Boil the water with the sugar, cinnamon and cloves for five minutes. Add the lemon slices and allow to stand for ten minutes. Add the wine and heat slowly but do not allow to boil. Serve very hot in pre-warmed glasses. Serves 8.

Wassail Bowl

6 pints brown ale	1 large cinnamon stick
½ pound soft brown sugar (or ½-1 cup US coffee sugar)	1 teaspoon grated nutmeg
	2 thinly sliced lemons
½ teaspoon ground ginger	2 roasted apples
	1 bottle inexpensive amontillado sherry

Pour 2 pints of the ale into a large saucepan, together with the sugar and cinnamon stick. Heat gently until the sugar has dissolved before adding all the other ingredients. Gradually bring the mixture to the boil. To impart an extra kick, add a glass of brandy just before serving. Serves 25-30.

William Henry Harrison's Egg Nog

1 egg
1½ teaspoons sugar
2 or 3 small lumps of ice
cider

Mix the egg, sugar and ice in a tumbler, then top up with cider. .
Serves 1.

Christmas Juice Punch

1½ pints (2 US pints)
   apple juice
1½ pints (2 US pints)
   cranberry juice
½ cup lemon juice
½ cup sugar
1 bottle ginger ale

Combine everything except the ginger ale and stir well. Just before serving add the ginger ale and some ice if desired.
Serves 15-20.

There's nothing like Father's Christmas Guinness except another Father's
Christmas Guinness

Christmas in the Antarctic

Thursday 25 December 1902 Christmas Day. Just gone midnight. A Merry Christmas to all at home. We are in our bags writing up diaries, looking forward to full meals for once. Turned out at 9 a.m. to a glorious Christmas of blazing sunshine. We were cooked by it all day, except while we were cooking. We had three hot meals! I read Holy Communion and various other things in my bag before we turned out.

Our meals must be given in detail as they were very exceptionally good today. I cooked the breakfast. We had tea, extra strong and sweet. (Milk of course we haven't had since we left the ship.) Biscuit, and a pannikin full of biscuit crumbs, bacon and seal liver fried up in pemmican. To top up we each had a spoonful of blackberry jam from a tin we brought specially for this day, our only tin.

After breakfast we grouped ourselves in front of the camp and let off the camera by a string, flying all our flags and the Union Jack. We then did a good 6 miles' march and camped for lunch in great heat. We had a brew of Bovril chocolate and plasmon [a protein supplement], biscuit and more blackberry jam. The Captain [Robert Falcon Scott] took a sight and I made a sketch, but my left eye is useless. We then did 4 miles and camped for the night at 8.30 p.m., having covered 10 miles in from 6 to 7 hours, a great improvement . . . .

Shackle cooked our supper. We had three NAO rations, with biscuit and a tomato soup square from our 'Hoosh McGoo'. Then a very small plum pudding, the size of a cricket ball, with biscuit and the remains of the blackberry jam and two pannikins of cocoa with plasmon. We meant to have had some brandy alight on the plum pudding, but all our brandy has turned black in its tin for some reason, so we left it alone. We enjoyed our Christmas, though so far from home.

DR EDWARD WILSON

Goodwill to Men:
Give us your Money

It was Christmas Eve on a Friday,
The shops was full of cheer,
With tinsel in the windows,
And presents twice as dear.
A thousand Father Christmases
Sat in their little huts,
And folk was buying crackers
And folk was buying nuts.

All up and down the country,
Before the light was snuffed,
Turkeys they got murdered,
And cockerels they got stuffed.
Christmas cakes got marzipanned,
And puddins they got steamed,
Mothers they got desperate,
And tired kiddies screamed.

Hundredweights of Christmas cards
Went flying through the post,
With first-class postage stamps on those
You had to flatter most.
Within a million kitchens,
Mince pies was being made,
On everybody's radio,
'White Christmas' it was played.

Out in the frozen countryside,
Men crept round on their own,
Hacking off the holly
What other folks had grown,
Mistletoe in willow trees
Was by a man wrenched clear,
So he could kiss his neighbour's wife
He'd fancied all the year.

And out upon the hillside
Where the Christmas trees had stood,
All was completely barren
But for little stumps of wood.
The little trees that flourished
All the year were there no more,
But in a million houses
Dropped their needles on the floor.

And out of every cranny, cupboard,
Hiding place and nook,
Little bikes and kiddies' trikes
Were secretively took.
Yards of wrapping paper
Was rustled round about,
And bikes were wheeled to bedrooms
With the pedals sticking out.

Rolled up in Christmas paper,
The Action Men were tensed,
All ready for the morning,
When their fighting life commenced.
With tommy guns and daggers,
All clustered round about,
'Peace on Earth – Goodwill to Men',
The figures seemed to shout.

The church was standing empty,
The pub was standing packed,
There came a yell, 'Noel, Noel!'
And glasses they got cracked.
From up above the fireplace,
Christmas cards began to fall,
And trodden on the floor, said:
'Merry Xmas, to you all.'

PAM AYRES

Something for Baby

Hang up the baby's stocking! Be sure
you don't forget! The dear little dim-
pled darling, she never saw Christmas
yet! But I've told her all about it, and
she opened her big blue eyes; and I'm sure
she understood it—she looked so funny
and wise. ∵ Dear, what a tiny stocking! It doesn't take much to hold such
little pink toes as baby's away from the
frost and cold. But then, for the baby's
Christmas, it will never do at all. Why!
Santa wouldn't be looking for anything
half so small. ∵ I know what will
do for the baby. I've thought of the
very best plan. I'll borrow a stocking of Grandma's, the longest
that ever I can. And you'll
hang it by mine, dear mother,
right here in the corner,
so! And leave a letter to
Santa, and fasten it on to
the toe. ∵ Write—this
is the baby's stocking,
that hangs in the corner
here. You never have
seen her, Santa, for she
only came this year.
But she's just the bless-
ed'st baby. And now
before you go, just cram
her stocking with
goodies, from the
top clean down
to the
toe!

W. F. DAWSON

Hospitality on the Road

The Rhine soon takes a sharp turn eastwards, and the walls of the valley recede again. I crossed the river to Rüdesheim, drank a glass of Hock under the famous vineyard and pushed on. The snow lay deep and crisp and even. On the march under the light fall of flakes, I wondered if I had been right to leave Bingen. My kind benefactors had asked me to stay, several times; but they had been expecting relations and, after their hospitality, I felt, in spite of their insistence, that a strange face at their family feast might be too much. So here I was on a sunny Christmas morning, plunging on through a layer of new snow. No vessels were moving on the Rhine, hardly a car passed, nobody was out of doors and, in the little towns, nothing stirred. Everyone was inside. Feeling lonely and beginning to regret my flight, I wondered what my family and my friends were doing, and skinned and ate the tangerine rather pensively. The flung peel, fallen short on the icy margin, became the target for a sudden assembly of Rhine gulls. Watching them swoop, I unpacked and lit one of my Christmas cigarettes, and felt better.

In the inn where I halted at midday – *where was it? Geisenheim? Winkel? Östrich? Hattenheim?* – a long table was splendidly spread for a feast and a lit Christmas tree twinkled at one end. About thirty people were settling down with a lot of jovial noise when some soft-hearted soul must have spotted the solitary figure in the empty bar. Unreluctantly, I was

drawn into the feast; and here, in my memory, as the bottles of Johannisberger and Markobrunner mount up, things begin to grow blurred.

A thirsty and boisterous rump at the end of the table was still drinking at sunset. Then came a packed motorcar, a short journey, and a large room full of faces and the Rhine twinkling far below. Perhaps we were in a castle... some time later, the scene changes: there is another jaunt, through the dark this time, with the lights multiplying and the snow under the tyres turning to slush; then more faces float to the surface and music and dancing and glasses being filled and emptied and spilled.

I woke up dizzily next morning on someone's sofa. Beyond the lace curtains and some distance below, the snow on either side of the tramlines looked unseasonably mashed and sooty for the feast of Stephen.

PATRICK LEIGH FERMOR

Christmas in Wartime

The Christmas shops have showed little shortage of the traditional delicacies, except turkeys, which are both scarce and expensive. The big stores came out valiantly with holly-and-cellophane-garlanded signs proclaiming that 'There'll always be a Christmas,' and did a rattling good trade in spite of the publicity campaign suggesting that a couple of National Savings Certificates in the toe of the stocking was all that any good citizen could need. Parents have taken advantage of the lull in the blitz to smuggle children up from the country for a brisk scurry through the toy bazaars, thereby brightening the lives of all the Santas, who had been drooping in their red flannelette and false whiskers among the childless acres of dolls and electric trains.

However unseasonably men may be behaving at this festival of peace on earth and mercy mild, the heavens are contributing a seasonable note. British astronomers are excited over what they call the triple conjunction of Jupiter and Saturn – a spectacle which was last seen in England when Charles II was on the throne and is recorded as one of the strange happenings preceding the birth of Christ. Londoners tacking up the holly in their Anderson shelters are hoping that this will be the only unusual display in the heavens when once more they celebrate that birth on the night of December 25th, 1940.

MOLLIE PANTER-DOWNES

Week ending December 21 1946   Every Thursday Threepence

JOHN BULL

J. B. PRIESTLEY
on "The Spirit of Christmas"
SEE PAGE 7

With all kind thoughts to distant friends this Christmas.

from

Walter Hayward

Colonial Christmas Day

Christmas dinner in Australia. Spread the cloth, spread it even, spread it smooth. But not on a polished table; spread it low and smooth beneath a gum trêe on the wiry grass. Dress it with red and yellow bells, Christmas bells on thin brown stalks.

What shall we eat for Christmas dinner in Australia? What do they eat thirteen thousand miles away in Sussex? Turkey and plum pudding – then we will eat it, too. Turkey cold in lettuce leaves, ice-cream from a thermos, plum pudding, not for eating, but for sixpences and sentiment, plum pudding shameless from a tin. Even Christmas dinner shall be casual, shall be happy-go-lucky in Australia.

Christmas dinner along the overland stock route across the continent. Sand and a million flies. Sand and flies and the mirage. Thin and blue the smoke of a billy fire drifting straight up in the windless air. Billy fire of an overlander, of a lean, lone overlander, Darwin-bound. Damper for his dinner, his Christmas dinner; but no regret for gayer Christmases seems to shadow his philosophic calm. Calm of philosophy, calm of solitude, calm of the desert, of the brooding grey-green bush. How should one so calm regret a tinsel day, a bon-bon day, like Christmas. Besides, having lost count of the days, he is under the impression that Christmas is still three days away.

JEAN CURLEWIS

The Christmas Air Raid

For some of us Christmas is an air raid from which we long to take cover. I've had seventy Christmases and seventy Christmas dinners, although the first was a bit sparse. The temptation of crouching under the staircase becomes annually stronger. That's not to say I don't love the family and the decorations and the presents and the visit of a very dear old friend who stipulates transport back to the Smoke on Boxing Day not later than five. Besides I'm the head of the family now since Gladys Cooper died, and there are responsibilities and the privilege of not having to carve the bird – not that I ever did. Delegate is the secret, let someone else lay the table and bring in the logs. In our house there are always willing hands – my wife's. By Christmas Eve she's absolutely exhausted. What if I were to go away next year – what if we both were to do so? There are hotels in Torquay which others patronize. The festivities are subdued and, even if they become embarrassingly hearty, there is the bedroom and even better the bed.... I suppose I could do something useful like scurrying around a hospital ward or relieving a traffic warden. Christmas is shorter for actors if they're working, two performances on Boxing Day, in New York two performances on Christmas Day itself. I suppose it's shorter too for priests, skeleton shift workers and Safari Park attendants. For most of us it's long enough. We begin to grow restless after the Queen's speech or when we wake from the afternoon nap to confront Billy Smart's circus ....

Of course, there are always the presents to play with. I've made my list and now we shall have to see. There is a clock which lights up when you clap your hands. It's called the slave clock and I saw it in New York but was too mean to buy it. I don't suppose it's reached these shores yet. I put in for some new executive toy, not a puzzle, I cannot do puzzles .... People will give me books on gambling and horse racing. I don't want to read them; when I can afford it I like to go in person to Sandown or a casino.

About the day after the day after Boxing Day my wife will ask me if I am going to put away the bath oil and the ties. I love bath oil but the ties I get seem to sting like those mysterious invisible fleas in the water off Bora Bora. The ties tend to depress me, I find myself worrying about the life style of the donors, they can't be happy I tell myself, they couldn't have been concentrating when they chose this one, there must be some awful gnawing secret sorrow of which I know nothing.

The grandchildren's presents are best, the tooth picks, the cloth to clean the lens of my spectacles, the chocolate orange. Then, of course, there's Daisy, my newest granddaughter. This will be her first Christmas and I am hoping for something really sensational from her. My present is a cot fitment from Sweden. If you fix it right, it converts her sleeping quarters into a sort of private gymnasium – I just hope she doesn't reciprocate with one of those appalling stationary bicycles.

ROBERT MORLEY

Behold a Rose is Springing

Behold a rose is springing
Upon this holy tree,
Our elders thus were singing
Of Jesse's line to be:
A rosebud pure and white
Deep in the cold midwinter
Upon the dark midnight.

This rose foretold in story
Springs as Isaiah said,
Bringing to us the glory
Of Mary perfect maid;
Through God's own power and might
Hath she brought forth her flower
Upon the dark midnight.

O hear us, gracious mother,
Sweet Mary, tender rose,
Through all thy Son did suffer,
His sorrows and his woes,
Help us prepare a bower
Within our hearts to cherish
This pure and perfect flower.

GERMAN CAROL TRANSLATED
BY IRIS HOLLAND ROGERS

MAY CHRISTMAS FIND·YOU·MERRY

THIS·COMES·TO·SAY
·A·GOOD·
OLD·FASHIONED·CHRISTMAS·DAY

A Memory of Love and Peace, 1626

It is now Christmas, and not a cup of drink must pass without a carol; the beasts, fowl and fish come to a general execution and the corn is ground to dust for the bakehouse, and the pastry. Cards and dice purge many a purse, and the youth shew their agility in shoeing of the wild mare....Musicians now make their instruments speak out, and a good song is worth the hearing. In sum, it is a holy time, a duty in Christians for the remembrance of Christ, and a custom among friends for the maintenance of good fellowship. In brief, I thus conclude of it: I hold it a memory of the heaven's love and the world's peace, the mirth of the honest, and the meeting of the friendly.

NICHOLAS BRETON

Celebrations at
Bracebridge Hall

We had not been long home when the sound of music
was heard from a distance. A band of country lads
without coats, their shirt sleeves fancifully tied with
ribands, their hats decorated with greens, and clubs in
their hands, were seen advancing up the avenue,
followed by a large number of villagers and peasantry.
They stopped before the hall door, where the music
struck up a peculiar air, and the lads performed a
curious and intricate dance, advancing, retreating,
and striking their clubs together, keeping exact time
to the music; while one, whimsically crowned with a
fox's skin, the tail of which flaunted down his back,
kept capering round the skirts of the dance, and
rattling a Christmas box with many antic gesticula-
tions.

The Squire eyed this fanciful exhibition with great
interest and delight, and gave me a full account of its
origin, which he traced to the times when the
Romans held possession of the island, plainly proving
that this was a lineal descendant of the sword dance
of the ancients. 'It was now,' he said, 'nearly extinct,
but he had accidentally met with traces of it in the
neighbourhood, and had encouraged its revival,
though, to tell the truth, it was too apt to be followed
up by rough cudgel play, and broken heads, in the
evening.'

After the dance was concluded, the whole party was

entertained with brawn and beef, and stout home brewed. The Squire himself mingled among the rustics, and was received with awkward demonstrations of deference and regard. It is true, I perceived two or three of the younger peasants, as they were raising their tankards to their mouths, when the Squire's back was turned, making something of a grimace, and giving each other the wink, but the moment they caught my eye they pulled grave faces, and were exceedingly demure. With Master Simon, however, they all seemed more at their ease....

The whole house indeed seemed abandoned to merriment: as I passed to my room to dress for dinner, I heard the sound of music in a small court, and looking through a window that commanded it, I perceived a band of wandering musicians with pandean pipes and tambourine: a pretty coquettish housemaid was dancing a jig with a smart country lad, while several of the other servants were looking on. In the midst of her sport the girl caught a glimpse of my face at the window, and colouring up, ran off with an air of roguish affected confusion.

WASHINGTON IRVING

Gifts for the Servants

Westmoreland County, Virginia
Saturday 25 December, 1773
Nelson the boy who makes my fire, blacks my shoes,
does errands etc was early in my room, dressed only in
his shirt and breeches! He made me a vast fire,
blacked my shoes, set my room in order, and wished
me a joyful Christmas, for which I gave him half a
Bit. Soon after he left the room, and before I was
dressed, the fellow who makes the fire in our school
room, dressed very neatly in green, but almost drunk,
entered my chamber with three or four profound
bows, and made me the same salutation; I gave him a
Bit, and dismissed him as soon as possible. Soon after
my clothes and linen were sent in with a message for
a Christmas Box, as they call it; I sent the poor slave
a Bit, and my thanks....I gave Tom the coachman,
who doctors my horse, for his care two Bits, and am
to give more when the horse is well. I gave to Dennis
the boy who waits at table half a Bit. So that the sum
of my donations to the servants for this Christmas
appears to be five Bits. (A Bit is a pisterene bisected,
or an English sixpence, and passes here for seven
pence halfpenny; the whole is 3s. 1½d)

PHILIP VICKERS FITHIAN

A Christmas Wish

May you have the gladness of Christmas, which is hope;
The spirit of Christmas, which is peace;
The heart of Christmas, which is love.

ADA V. HENDRICKS

I'VE BROUGHT A CHRISTMAS KISS FOR THEE,
STOOP DOWN AND TAKE IT PRAY FROM ME

Answers to the Christmas Quiz. 1 Charles Dickens' *A Christmas Carol*.
2 *Twelfth Night* and *Hamlet*. 3 Punch, because it is meant to have five
ingredients. 4 When Apollo 8 orbited the Moon in 1968 the astronauts took
turns to read out extracts from Genesis. 5 December means tenth not twelfth
month, the name dating from the old Roman calendar. 6 The turkey, which was
brought to Europe from America. 7 Clement C. Moore, who wrote ''Twas the
Night Before Christmas' whereas George R. Sims wrote 'Christmas Day in the
Workhouse'. 8 They are said to represent gold, frankincense and myrrh. 9 Its
charms is an anagram of Christmas.

Acknowledgements

For permission to reproduce copyright material the publishers thank the following:
Rosalind Wade; Hamish Hamilton Ltd and Random House Inc for 'A Childhood
Expedition' from 'A Christmas Memory' by Truman Capote; Jonathan Cape Ltd for
the extract from Kilvert's diary edited by William Plomer; Edwin Morgan and
Carcanet Press Ltd for 'The Computer's First Christmas Card'; Pam Ayres and
Dolphin Concert Productions Ltd for 'Goodwill to Men: Give Us Your Money'; The
Scott Polar Research Institute, University of Cambridge, for the extract from the
diary of Edward Wilson as edited by Harry King and published in *South Pole Odyssey*
(Blandford Press, 1982); John Fairfax and Sons Ltd for 'Colonial Christmas Day'
from *Christmas in Australia* by Jean Curlewis (Art in Australia, 1928); Laurence
Pollinger Ltd and Farrar, Straus & Giroux Inc for 'Christmas in Wartime' from
London War Notes 1939-45 by Mollie Panter-Downes; Hughes Massie Ltd for 'Carol
of the Brown King' by Langston Hughes; Constable and Co and the Savoy Hotel for
the recipe of General Harrison's Egg Nog from *The Savoy Cocktail Book*; Robson
Books Ltd for 'The Christmas Air Raid' from *Morley Matters* by Robert Morley; Lord
Horder for 'Behold a Rose is Springing' from *The Orange Carol Book* (Schott, 1972);
Oxford University Press for 'Wassail, Wassail, all Over the Town' from *The Oxford
Book of Carols*; John Murray (Publishers) Ltd for 'Hospitality on the Road' from *A
Time of Gifts* by Patrick Leigh Fermor; University Press of Virginia for 'Gifts for the
Servants' from *Journal and Letters of Philip Vickers Fithian, 1773-1774* (Colonial
Williamsburg Inc, 1945); Miss D. E. Collins for 'A Child of the Snows' by G. K.
Chesterton; Jane MacQuitty and *The Times* for the Wassail Bowl recipe. The extract
from the Authorized King James Version of The Bible, which is Crown Copyright in
the UK, is reproduced by permission of Eyre & Spottiswoode, Her Majesty's
Printers, London. 'Goose for the Cratchits' is taken from *A Christmas Carol* by
Charles Dickens; 'Celebrations at Bracebridge Hall' comes from *The Sketch Book of
Geoffrey Crayon, Gent* by Washington Irving; and 'A Memory of Love and Peace,
1626' by Nicholas Breton is taken from *Fantastickes* (1626). For permission to
reproduce illustrations we thank the following: The Victoria and Albert Museum;
The Scott Polar Research Institute of Cambridge for the sketch by Edward Wilson;
Sonia Halliday and Laura Lushington; Syndication International; Arthur Guinness
and Son Ltd; Lindley Library, Royal Horticultural Society; Bridgeman Art Library;
Marcel Ashby. We also wish to thank the following for their help: Nicky Bowden;
Westminster City Libraries; Godfrey New Photographics Ltd; Chris Davies; The
British Newspaper Library; and Larry. The Publishers wish all the readers of this
book a very happy Christmas.